I0782225

Grandmother's Cottage

Sylvia Pelton Kroll

Stories
Grandmother's Cottage

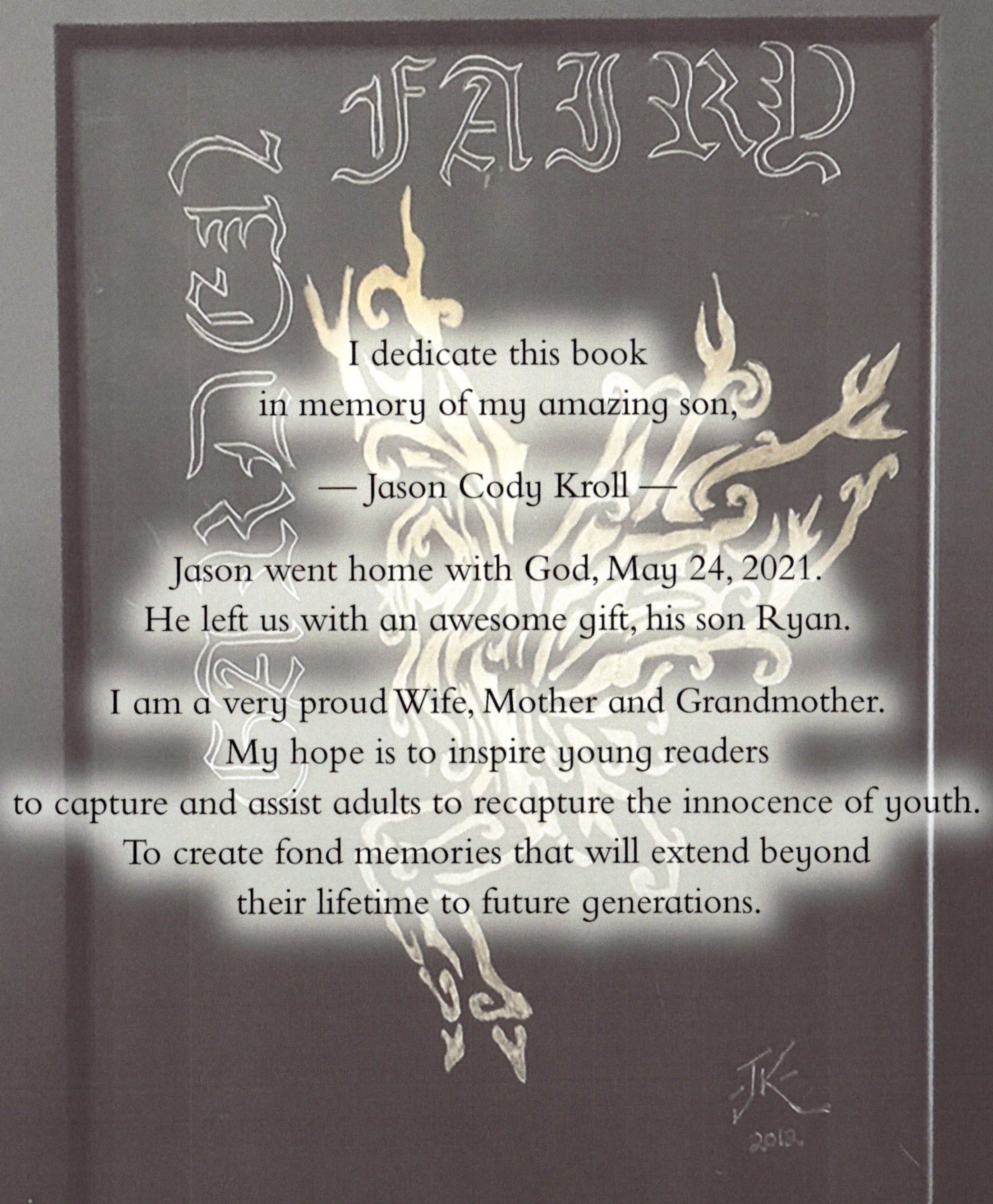

I dedicate this book
in memory of my amazing son,

— Jason Cody Kroll —

Jason went home with God, May 24, 2021.
He left us with an awesome gift, his son Ryan.

I am a very proud Wife, Mother and Grandmother.
My hope is to inspire young readers
to capture and assist adults to recapture the innocence of youth.
To create fond memories that will extend beyond
their lifetime to future generations.

INTRODUCTION

As I shared this story with my son
I could easily tell the moment he had begun

To allow himself to be swept away
Behind Grandmothers cottage, just beyond the bay

Into the garden he did tread
Taken there by the words I read

Now I wish to share this view
In hopes that along with us, you too

Can you see the beauty that awaits you there?
Don't be surprised to find fairy dust in your hair.

So come now, let us read
Of the Garden Fairy and her good deeds.

GRANDMOTHER AND FRIENDS

Behind my grandmother's cottage,
just beyond the bay
There lived a garden fairy,
with whom I would spend many a day
She would delight me with stories,
in her enchanting way
Of how with the butterflies
and bees she would play

And effortlessly she would coax the flowers in their beds
To lift up their dreamy-sleepy heads
A kaleidoscope of color, beauty beyond compare
Then she would reach down and tousle my hair
With a gentle touch,
ever so light
I would giggle with laughter at that little sprite

10

The bees in the garden as you know
Often are very plentiful
There were two that always came
To listen to the stories and play our games
Steffie and Maxx were their names

Steffie had an artful flair
She was always buzzing around Garden Fairies hair
Trying as she thought she must
To shake out the extra fairy dust

Creating a new style, she thought was divine
A shiver of excitement ran down my spine
For I knew in a moment she would be
Repeating that same style on me

Then little Maxx would be a clown
Dancing about in one of Garden Fairies gowns

Next the butterflies would take flight
    Oh what a beautiful sight
For the rest of us in the garden to behold
As we listened to the stories the Garden Fairy told

They would flutter about without a care

            Almost weightless, seeming lighter than air
            Drifting about for hours
            Dancing around us, and the flowers

They told us of how some were captured by nets
But not for long, as you can bet
            For they would find a way to break free
            As God intended them to be

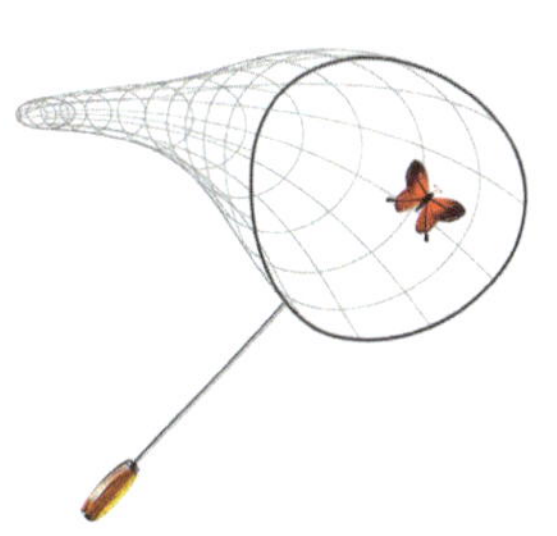

14

In the garden there also
lived a bunny
He was really cute and
very funny

He would nibble on the
flowers, thinking we could
not see

And try to get our
attention away from the
butterflies and the bees

Timidly, he would come
closer to hear
He knew from us he had
nothing to fear

The stories the Garden Fairy would tell
Kept us entranced in a spell
Of pure contentment and delight
Then as daylight gave way to night
We knew it was time to leave
And as I wiped a tear with my sleeve

I realized I never wanted her to go away
Please stay I would say
But, as like all other fairies, fly she must
And as I glimpsed the last shimmer of fairy dust

I listened intently, and what I heard Miss Garden Fairy say
Was, I think we've all had enough play
Let's settle down now, night has begun
We'll wake tomorrow with the sun
And oh, what treasures we will find
In the garden right here behind
Grandmother's cottage

So, hurry on home, snuggle in tight
Have a peaceful restful night

It wasn't so long ago, or so far away
I was the child that would play
Behind my Grandmother's cottage, just beyond the bay

As I recall, I was barely three
When the Garden Fairy told her stories to me
I was quite enchanted back then
And if the truth be known, I still am

GRANDMOTHER AND GARDEN FAIRY BECOME FRIENDS

Memories are precious glimpses of the past to behold
Among my precious memories are the stories Garden Fairy told
Of these I have a favorite few
I would like to share with you

The first of these is when
She and Grandmother became friends

It was uncharacteristically cold that night
When Garden Fairy was beckoned by the light

To the window she had fled
Of the cottage where Grandmother lived

She was pressed tightly against the window pane
Trying to shelter herself from the freezing rain

Grandmother suddenly noticed her there
As she glanced outside, while brushing her hair

She approached the window with caution, as she tried
To convince Garden Fairy to come inside

You could see the hesitation etched in the glass
As her wings began to flutter fast

And her breath caught momentarily in her chest
As she asked herself, could I just
Join her for a short while?

She stole a glance, and caught Grandmother's smile
And in that moment, she knew it would be okay
To go inside, she didn't plan to stay
They chatted for what seemed like hours
Then Garden Fairy said, "Oh my, I must tend the flowers!"

Some are quite hearty, and will survive
But others will find it hard to stay alive
With a frost this heavy I fear
Grandmother said, "Your right my dear

I'll get my coat and join you
I think together we two
Can shelter them from the storm
I'll grab some blankets to keep them warm"

They spent half the night out there
Tending to the flowers with such care

When they had done all they could
They felt it to be best, if they would
Go back inside to the warmth of the fire
There for the evening they would retire

The friendship that started that night
Has like Garden Fairy, taken flight
Soaring to the Heavens above
Passed on to me and to you with love

THE SAND CASTLE

Another story Garden Fairy would tell
Was among the several I liked so well
It began with the sunrise on the bay
Which often found Grandmother and her at the water's edge to play

Garden Fairy had an enormous amount of curiosity
And with Grandmothers help she was able to see
The abundance of shells that washed to the shore
Left behind from the storm the night before

As Grandmother knelt down to scoop up some sand
Garden Fairy exclaimed, that looks like fairy dust in your hand,
The way it shimmers and sparkles in the light."
Grandmother said, "You know you're right.
Let's fill our buckets and go up on the beach
To where the water cannot reach.
We'll build a castle, you will see

And oh what a beauty it will be.
We'll have to add some water to pack it tight
So it will last through the night."

They worked on the castle throughout the day
Then Garden Fairy heard Grandmother say,

"I think our project is done
Just in time, for there goes the sun."

They walked back to the cottage with the light of the moon
Knowing they would awaken soon

And how they would rush through their chores
So they could return to the shore

Would their castle still be standing there?
I held my breath in fear

Many changes take place while we sleep
Was it allowed for them to keep
The castle standing bright and tall
Or in the night did it fall?

To the beach they ran hand in hand
What did they find on the sand?

A sigh of relief you too let out
It's here it's here they began to shout

Grandmother said, "I think we better,
add a little sand and water,

We will have to work fast
If we want our castle to last."

So, they rolled up their sleeves
And would you believe
In no time at all
They had built another wall

In place of the castle, a fortress now stood
Garden Fairy asked Grandmother, "Do you think I could,
fly inside and take a look around?"
All of a sudden, they heard a rumbling sound

It seems the storm from the night before
Decided to return once more

To the cottage Grandmother and Garden Fairy ran
Back in its safety once again

Isn't it wonderful to feel safe and warm?
To have a place to run, out of the storm.
We all have this ability
If we will open our eyes and see
It's all part of God's plan
For us to be a friend to our fellow man

32
Darky

THE WISHING WELL

I have another story which to you
I would like to tell
It's about Grandmother's wish
Spoken into the wishing well
As Garden Fairy told me,
I will tell you
Can you guess what happened?
Do you have a clue?

It was Grandmother's market day
But, as always Garden Fairy wanted to play.
She was dawdling about, while getting dressed
I had to laugh, I must confess

With a hint of irritation, Grandmother said,
"Hurry now and put a hat on your head
there's a chill in the air,
and after Steffie's styling you have very little hair.
We don't want you to get sick, do we?"
With that Garden Fairy had to agree.
She had too many things she wanted to do
To allow herself to be stuck in bed with the flu.

They got into the car, and as Grandmother drove
Garden Fairy would watch for danger in the road
She warned Grandmother to be careful, as there was a lot of debris
Branches and leaves that had fallen from the trees
Strewn about from the storm
She snuggled closer to Grandmother to keep warm

They arrived safely to the market, and when they were done
Grandmother said to Garden Fairy, "Shall we have some fun?"
Let's go to the park, "Did I hear you say?"
Grandmother said, "I guess it's not too far out of our way."

When they got to the park, it began to rain
Grandmother told Garden Fairy, "Now let's not complain.
"We can get an umbrella, and go for a walk,
and share our ideas while we talk."

As they walked, they suddenly found
A pile of pennies on the ground
Grandmother said, "I wonder where these came from,
we'll stop at the park station, and ask someone.

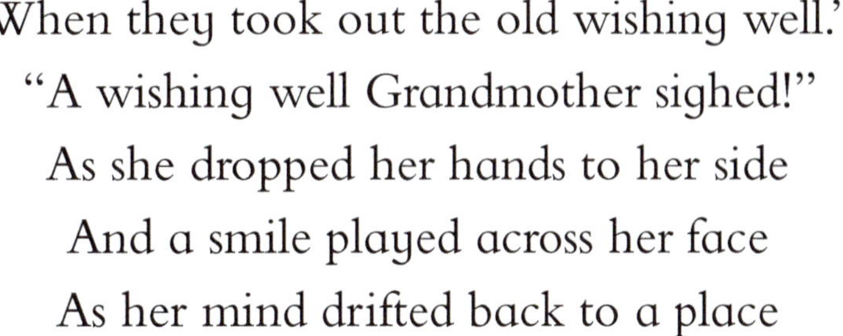

The attendant said, "They must have fell
When they took out the old wishing well."
"A wishing well Grandmother sighed!"
As she dropped her hands to her side
And a smile played across her face
As her mind drifted back to a place

When she cast her penny in with the rest
What do you think was her request?
Was it for a great fortune to come her-way?
Or perhaps a handsome prince to save the day?
I know the wish she wished came true
When I look around, and see all of you
Sharing, along with me
The stories in her memory.

STEFFIE AND MAXX GET CAUGHT

I've come to visit with you again
I hope by now you call me your friend
This story is very special to me
It's about those two silly bees
You remember Steffie and Maxx, don't you?
It seems they found themselves stuck in the toe of
Grandmothers shoe!

You can imagine the panic that began
When Grandmother tried putting her foot in

Garden Fairy laughed so hard; she fell to the ground
As she watched Grandmother dancing around

Grandmother said, "I'm trying my best to get off my shoe
Without hurting either one of you."

Garden Fairy said, "Let me help."
Just then Grandmother began to yelp!

It seems she had irritated little Maxx
And in defense, he stung her back.

At long last, she managed to get her foot free
Garden Fairy flitted about, trying to see.

Making sure everyone stayed calm
Assuring little Maxx he had done no harm.

Grandmother said, "I'll be okay you two
Now what was I trying to do?"
"It seems I lost my train of thought,
By the way, how did you two get caught?"

As she laughed, her head began to shake
She said, "What a spectacle the four of us make,
We better get busy now and carry on,
With the chores, we must get done."
The fence in the garden needs repair,
Let's all go outside for some fresh air."

They were all still laughing, as they marched outside
Garden Fairy asked Grandmother,

"If I get in the wagon, will you take me for a ride?"
Grandmother said. "I may as well take all of you."
She looked at Steffie and Maxx, and said, "Come on you two."

They all had so much fun that day
Even though it started in a funny way.

I'm sure, like me, there have been
moments in your life,
When you feel overcome with strife.

Here is a saying, I want you to know,
"God never closes a door, that he doesn't open a window."

Our moments of pleasure, are the seeds we sow
In our garden of life they will grow.
I hope you have a garden full
And that your life is wonderful!

MR. BUNNY IN A BIND

I have another story to add to the rest
I promise you it won't be my last

Oh pardon me, I just had to sneeze
Is it possible I'm allergic to bunnies?

Did I hear you say, "It can't be that?"
Perhaps you're right, it must be from the cat!

Do you remember the bunny in Grandmother's
garden being timid and shy?
He no longer is, and let me tell you why.

Grandmother heard a scared little voice say,
"I'm over here, please come help me."

As she was planting some flowers, she had just bought
You see, it seems Mr. Bunny got himself caught.

While hopping around contentedly
Some leftover twine, he did not see.

He was really in a bind
Grandmother said, "I will help you if you don't mind."

He sat very still, not really sure
If he could put his trust in Grandmother

We all know how gentle she is, and that he would be in good hands
But poor Mr. Bunny's insides were like rubber bands
Tight from the tension, he felt he would burst
Grandmother asked Garden Fairy to run and fetch her purse.

She needed a pair of scissors, and a band-aid just in case
You can imagine the look on Mr. Bunny's face

It was priceless, as you can understand
Garden Fairy said, "Don't be scared, I'll hold your hand."

When at last they set him free
It was he that decided he wanted to be part of their family
Grandmother said, "Now you must not be shy,
Listen closely, and I will tell you why."

"In the Garden we all have to be willing and able to help each other out
So before you agree, make sure you have no doubts."

The others nodded in agreement as
Grandmother spoke
They knew what she was saying was no joke.

There is a degree of danger everywhere you go
I've heard it said, it's how the wind blows,
Or the shape of the moon, or how you wear your hat.
I don't know if I agree with all of that.
But, this much I know is true,
When you put your trust in God, he will protect you.
Even when your hurt, and he can't come
He will always provide for you, and send someone.

SEARCHING FOR TREASURE

Grandmother would sit on her front porch in her rocking chair
Across the bay, to the distant shore she would stare
Watching the tide approach and recede
Leaving behind tiny treasures in the seaweed

She went to her kitchen, and there she would don
What she fondly referred to as, her gathering apron
Why did she call it that, did you ask?
Because it had lots of pockets, for many a task

Today she would use it on the shore
The treasures she would find, in the pockets she would store

She went quickly down the steps to be on her way
As she walked towards the garden you could hear her say,
"Does anyone want to go with me, I'm headed for the bay?"

They all began talking at once
Can you guess what they said, do you have a hunch?

I probably don't have to tell you, I'm sure you already know
The answer was unanimous, they all wanted to go!

Laughing with excitement, from the garden they ran out
"Wait for me," Garden Fairy began to shout

She was primping in the gazing ball, admiring her hair
For the amount of time she was spending, she hadn't a care

It was early morning, and she had nothing planed
But she couldn't resist the invitation to play in the sand

I know you would want to be included in this too
And you would stop what you were doing, wouldn't you?
Even if giving up on extra primping was what it meant
Wouldn't spending time with your friends, be time better spent?

We all have to make choices each and every day
As for this choice, I would have to say
Go for it! The primping can wait
You'll get enough of that when you're old enough to date.

THE FISHING TRIP

Did you know that Grandmother had a boat?
Sure she did, you ask "Could it float?"

It was weathered and old, but as Grandmother would say, it was sound
Then she would chuckle as she remembered when she ran it aground

That's a term boaters say
When like Grandmother they get to close to the bay

They find they haven't shut the motor down
When all at once they hear a choking sound
Then suddenly the motor stops
And they feel the boat began to drop

They feel silly for what they have done
And know fixing the problem they have caused will be no fun

But let's get back to a happier thought
We'll tell of how they all went fishing and the fish they caught

Have you ever gone fishing, and caught the biggest one?
Do you remember the excitement, wasn't it fun?

Well, that my friend is the experience Mr. Bunny wants to tell you about
And how very special at that moment he felt

He had to sit quietly; for a very long time
Then all of a sudden there was a tug on his line

At first, he wasn't quite sure what to do
He heard, "Reel it in," from the rest of the crew
Ever so gently, he began
It was a struggle to reel it in

You see Mr. Bunny is not very large
And as fish stories go, it would have covered a barge
With the others help, he got it on board

Grandmother said, "Will it fit in the ice chest? "It'll have to be stored,
Until we get home, let's be on our way,
We'll have it for dinner, what do you say?"

To this suggestion, Mr. Bunny made the reply,
"We have to eat it, why?"

The rest of the crew let out a shout
"Did you think we were just going to toss it out?"

Grandmother said, "Come now I'll let you help me,
It'll make a fine meal, you will see,
We'll add some potatoes and carrots form the garden."
"UMM, Carrots!", Mr. Bunny said with a grin

That's when he decided it would be okay
To cook the fish he caught that day.

Like Mr. Bunny, I have to agree,
Eating fish doesn't really excite me.
Isn't it nice to be able to choose what we want to eat?
Whether it be fruit or vegetable, bread or meat?
God has given us an abundance of all of them
Whatever we choose, matters not to him

When you fill your plate, I hope you haven't forgot
As Grandmother would say, "Waste not want not."

BLUE GOOSE

In this story, to you I would like to introduce
Our feathered friend, we fondly refer to as, Blue Goose
What's that you say, you never heard of a goose that was blue?
Well then, my dear, I have a surprise for you.

I must confess that was not how she was hatched
In fact she was white like the rest of the batch

Are you curious then, of how she became blue?
Why this happened, I will gladly share with you.

Have you heard the story of the ugly duckling that became a swan?
And how the others could not believe it was the same one?

Well, for Blue Goose this happened in reverse
For as I told you, she was born white at first.

You see Blue Goose loved the bay
So much in fact, in the water was where she would stay

At first her color change was hardly noticeable
It was a shade of blue that was quite subtle

It was greatly enhanced by the light
From the sun during the day and the moon at night

It happened to her gradually
Grandmother said it was from spending so much time in the sea

Blue Goose didn't see it quite that way
She felt like an outcast, and didn't want to play
We told her she was radiant
She would shrug and say she didn't know what that meant

We explained to her that when she would fly
As the light caught her wings, she would brighten the sky
What was that, you didn't know geese flew?
Then for today, I guess you have learned "Your something new"
It's said, "We learn something new every day"
Must be true, what do you say?

Have you ever felt like Blue Goose, and couldn't understand
Why you somehow felt, that with the others, you didn't quite fit in?
Let me share something with you, my friend
We are all here, as part of Gods plan.
On this earth we all have a purpose and a place
It takes all of us together to make the human race
So be a beacon and let your light shine through
Don't worry what others might think about you
In Gods eyes, we are all beautiful!

THE HUMMINGBIRD

They were sitting in the garden, enjoying their tea
When they both saw something quite suddenly
It left as quickly as it appeared
Grandmother told Garden Fairy,
"That was a hummingbird."
Garden Fairy asked, "A hummingbird did you say?
From what I saw of it, it was very pretty."

Grandmother said, "We'll put out a feeder for it and then,
We'll be able to see it better when it comes again."

As Grandmother tried to describe to Garden Fairy
how a feeder should look
She stopped herself and said, "Wait a minute, I'm sure I have a book
Ah yes, but it's more like a catalog actually."
As she wiped off the dust it had gathered while sitting
on a shelf in the library.

Garden Fairy was anxious for her to get to the page so she could see
Do you think there was a picture of the hummingbird, well just maybe.

They were turning the pages, when Grandmother said, with a grin,
"Look over there, he's back again."

"Oh!" Garden Fairy exclaimed with delight
"Do you think we could get a closer look, without giving him a fright?"

Grandmother said, "We better go into town to see if we can find
A feeder for him, I have a store in mind."

When they returned, they put the feeder up
The hummingbird began feeding immediately,
he didn't seem to want to stop.

Garden Fairy whispered to Grandmother, "He must really be hungry."
Grandmother replied, "Well, he has been feeding steadily,
I wonder if he has a mate,
Who's waiting somewhere wondering why he is so late?"

Garden Fairy said, "Oh Grandmother you are a funny gal,
That's one of the things I love about being your pal!
Perhaps he'll bring his mate when he returns
To help erase any of her concerns
Regarding his story, of why he was tardy,
We could invite them to our tea party."
Grandmother said, "That's a splendid idea,
your so clever!"
Then into the house she went,
for the extra tea cups and saucers
she had to gather.

Together they all had tea
And enjoyed each other's company.

Doesn't that sound like fun?
Sharing what you have to offer with someone
Who was just a stranger a moment ago
But now is a friend you've gotten to know.

THE SECRET PARTY

Well now my little friend
As you know, every story must have an end

So, let's gather all our friends to Grandmother's cottage
just beyond the bay
Into the garden for the day

Grandmother has been quite sick
So we'll all have to help, and make it quick

There will be the hummingbird couple,
Mr. Bunny and Blue Goose, and
Steffie and Maxx, we can't forget those two
And yes, my friend, I've included you.

Now let me see,
Do you think I forgot anybody?

What was that you say?
I left out Miss Garden Fairy!

Shh, we must not let our secret out
For Grandmother and her are what our surprise is all about

I know it will be hard not to tell
But, if it leaks out, it will spoil the surprise for them as well

We'll have to plan a menu of what we want to eat
Did I hear Mr. Bunny volunteer to bring the meat?

Okay, I guess for this day we can do fish
Grandmother thinks it makes a very fine dish

Blue Goose said she could spare some eggs
And for our fruit, the hummingbird couple said they would bring figs

Oh yes, and carrots for our vegetable from Mr. Bunny
Guess the rest is left to you and me

If it's alright with you, I'll bring the cake
I know just the kind I want to bake

I'll use petals from the flowers to decorate
I'm so excited, I can hardly wait

I'll have to decide on what to wear
Do you think I should ask Steffie to do my hair?
Was that a giggle, as you replied?
You'll never know until you've tried

Although what you've said, my friend, may be true,
"I'd rather she practices on someone else, how about you?"

GRANDMOTHER'S PASSING

I'm feeling quite sad today
As sometime during the night, Grandmother passed away

Did I hear you say, "What does that mean?"
For you little one, I'll try to explain
In a way that I hope you can understand
In hope that you too, can pass it on to a friend

When someone we love is taken away
For their quick return, we often pray

It's hard for us to say goodbye
That's why my dear, we often cry

When we think we can no longer see their face
Or share the warmth of their embrace

It makes us feel very sad
When in a way, we should be glad
For when they pass onto Heaven, to live with God
We need to remember, we still have their love

All you really have to do
Is remember them, and they are there with you

Remember the scent of the clothes they wore
And suddenly you're with then once more

I'm sure you can even see their face
And feel the warmth of their embrace
"That's easy," did I hear you say?
Now go outside with your friends and play

I know your loved one wouldn't want to see
You sitting around feeling sorry
With a long face and a heavy heart
Of this they would want to be no part

ABOUT THE AUTHOR

Sylvia Pelton Kroll is originally from Clare, Michigan. She currently lives in Litchfield Park, Arizona with her husband Rod. Due to Rod's military career of twenty-two years, she was given a great opportunity to not only travel, but to experience different cultures and lifestyles around the world, which has allowed her to develop many skills. Her ability to create a lighthearted yet thought-provoking use of imagination has helped her to discover a talent for writing which allows the reader to embrace the magic of childhood.